Hairy Maclary, Shoo

Lynley Dodd

PUFFIN

Hairy Maclary
was having some fun,
messing about
with his friends
in the sun.
Frisky and skittish,
they romped
and they ran,
when . . .

up came a dusty
delivery van.
Off went the driver
with cartons of soup
SO
Hairy Maclary
decided to
snoop.

Back came the driver
and SLAM went the door.
Off went the van
with a rattle and roar;
way past the park
and the slippery slide,
uphill
and downhill –
with Hairy
inside.

Round every corner
they wobbled and bopped
till,
far from the Dairy,
they finally stopped.
One parcel more
for a furniture store
BUT
Hairy Maclary
shot out of the door.

Into a toyshop
he skidded and spun,
scattering blocks
as he slid on his tum.
Teddy bears tumbled
and fell on his head,
all in a jumble,
till somebody said . . .

'STOP this shemozzle,
this hullabaloo!
Scarper,
skedaddle,
BE OFF WITH YOU –
SHOO!'

Straight through the gate
of Magnolia School,
raced Hairy Maclary
round playground and pool.
Through every classroom
he wickedly sped
till,
outside his office,
the headmaster
said . . .

'STOP this shemozzle,
this hullabaloo!
Scarper,
skedaddle,
BE OFF WITH YOU –
SHOO!'

Over to Gulliver's
Garden Supplies,
rushed Hairy Maclary
with scaredy-cat eyes.
Tangled in creepers,
he panicked and fled
through palm trees
and poppies,
till everyone said . . .

'STOP this shemozzle,
this hullabaloo!
Scarper,
skedaddle,
BE OFF WITH YOU –
SHOO!'

Hairy Maclary
was tired of the fun.
His whiskers were draggled,
his collar undone.
He hid between flowerpots,
sad and alone,
waiting for someone
to show the way
home.
Wearily woeful
and gloomily glum,
he gave a deep sigh –
then . . .

along came Miss Plum.
'It's HAIRY MACLARY –
good gracious!'
she said,
scooping him up
with a pat on his head.
'My,
what a raggedy rascal you are,'
she laughed
as she trundled him
out to her car.

A wag of his tail
and a fidgety toe
meant Hairy Maclary
was ready
to go.

He watched as they drove
over Butterfly Bridge,
up the long hill
over Rolla ay Ridge,
down r the park
        s zigzaggy bends,
back to the Dairy . . .